Pirate
Girl

First published in Germany by Verlag Friedrich Oetinger, Hamburg © 2003

This edition first published in the United Kingdom in 2005 by The Chicken House,
2 Palmer Street, Frome, Somerset, BA11 1DS
www.doublecluck.com
This edition published in 2006

Text © 2003 Cornelia Funke
Illustrations © 2003 Kerstin Meyer
English translation © 2005 Chantal Wright

Colour Reproduction by Dot Gradations Ltd, UK
Printed and bound in Singapore

British Library Cataloguing in Publication Data available
Library of Congress Cataloguing in Publication data available

ISBN 978 1 904442 93 6

Pirate Girl

by Cornelia Funke
Illustrated by Kerstin Meyer
Translated by Chantal Wright

Chicken House

2 Palmer Street, Frome, Somerset BA11 1DS

Captain Firebeard was the terror of the high seas. His ship, the Horrible Haddock, sailed faster than the wind over the waves. Whenever the Horrible Haddock appeared on the horizon, the knees of honest seafaring folk would shake like jelly.

Captain Firebeard had a fearsome crew. His helmsman was Morgan O'Meany. His cook was Cutlass Tom. Not forgetting Bill the Bald, Willy Wooden Hand, Crooked Carl and twenty more terrible pirates just like them.

When Firebeard's crew boarded a ship, nothing was safe. They stole the silver spoons and the captain's uniform. They stole the ship's figurehead, the pots and pans, the hammocks and the sails. And, of course, they stole ALL the casks of rum.

But one day Firebeard robbed a ship that he should have left well alone. On board was a little girl called Molly. Molly was off on holiday to see her granny.

The pirates leapt on board with an ear-splitting roar. Molly tried hiding among the ropes, but Morgan O'Meany soon fished her out.

'What shall we do with her?' he smirked.

'Take her with us, you fool!' bellowed Firebeard. 'Her parents will pay a handsome ransom for such a little treasure. And if not, then we'll feed her to the sharks.'

'You'll be sorry for this!' cried Molly.

But Morgan O'Meany rolled her up like a herring and tossed her on board the Horrible Haddock.

When the sun had gone down Bill the
Bald dragged Molly to see the captain.
'Right, tell me your parents' names and
address, or else!' growled Captain Firebeard.

'Will not!' Molly growled back. 'If I told you my mother's name, you'd be so scared, you'd cry like a baby!'

At this, all the pirates howled with laughter.

So Molly was put to work. She peeled potatoes and cleaned boots. She polished cutlasses, patched sails and scrubbed the deck. Soon every bone in her body ached.

Three times a day Firebeard asked her,
'Name and address?' But Molly just smiled.
  'Feed her to the sharks!' roared Willy
Wooden Hand. But Firebeard ground his
teeth and said, 'She'll talk before long.'

Every night the pirates had a party. They drank rum, staggered across the deck, danced on the ship's rigging and bawled out the rudest songs.

But Molly had a plan. While the pirates were carousing, she wrote secret messages and popped them into empty bottles. When the pirates were safely snoring in their bunks, she tossed them into the sea. Molly did this every night.

One night the pirates partied
until dawn. But this time, they
fell asleep on the deck.

Molly tiptoed over the tangle
of arms and legs, and threw her
bottle over the ship's rail.
Splish! Splash! It landed in the
deep, wide sea.

'Hey! What was that?' yelled Morgan O'Meany.
The pirates staggered over to the rail.

'It's a message in a bottle!' they all cried.

'Bring it to me!' shouted Captain Firebeard. 'Now!'

The pirates dived to the bottom of the sea. They searched and searched, but Molly's message had bobbed away. Soaking wet, they crawled back on deck, cursing.

'Tell me what you wrote!' demanded Captain Firebeard.

But Molly just kicked at his wooden leg.

Firebeard went as red as a lobster. 'NOW it's time to feed her to the sharks!' he roared.

But a cry from above stopped him.

'P. . .P. . .P. . . Pirates!'

shouted Ten-Pint Ted from the crow's nest.

'Nonsense!' scoffed Firebeard. '*We're* the only pirates around here.'

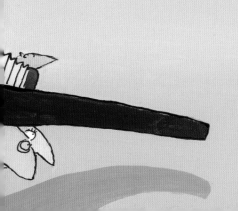

But he was wrong. A ship with red sails was speeding towards them. A giant black flag with a skull and crossbones fluttered from its mast.

'Who in the name of Neptune's beard is that?' stuttered Firebeard.

'That's my mum!' grinned Molly.

'It's Barbarous Bertha herself!' wailed the crew of the Horrible Haddock.

Firebeard went as white as a sheet and his pirates rolled their eyes in fear. This time, it was *their* knees that were shaking.

And Bill the Bald's false teeth almost flew out of his mouth.

The ship with the red sails drew closer and closer. Barbarous Bertha stood at the prow, swinging her cutlass.

'Wait until she sees my hands!' said Molly. 'They're red and raw from peeling potatoes. That will make my mum maddest of all!'

Firebeard and his pirates groaned with terror.

Soon Barbarous Bertha was alongside the Horrible Haddock. Her ferocious crew swung themselves over the rail with a terrible roar.

'We're here at last, my pirate girl!' cried Barbarous Bertha, throwing Molly up high into the air.

'We got your message. Your granny was beginning to wonder where you were. Now, how nasty can we be to these piratical nincompoops?'

'Well!' said Molly. 'That's easy.'

From that day on, Captain Firebeard and his pirate crew had no time to think about raiding ships.

Willy Wooden Hand scrubbed the deck.

Morgan O'Meany and Cutlass Tom peeled vegetables from morning until night.

Captain Firebeard polished Barbarous Bertha's boots fourteen times a week.

And Molly was finally able to visit her granny!

Born in Dorsten, Germany in 1958, *Cornelia Funke* has been writing and illustrating books for children since 1987.
She is the author of two international best-sellers, *Inkheart* and *The Thief Lord*, both published by The Chicken House.

Kerstin Meyer was born in Wedel near Hamburg in 1966. She studied illustration at Hamburg College of Design. Since taking her diploma in 1993 she has worked as an illustrator for several publishers of children's books as well as for television.